Hello CavMan!

Aimee Aryal

Illustrated by Gerry Perez

www.mascotbooks.com

It was a beautiful fall day at the
University of Virginia.

CavMan was on his way to Scott Stadium to watch a football game.

He walked onto the Lawn.

Some students walking by waved,
"Hello CavMan!"

CavMan stopped in front of Cabell Hall.

A professor walked past and said,
"Hello CavMan!"

CavMan walked over to Newcomb Hall
to meet some friends.

A group of UVA fans standing outside
said, "Hello CavMan!"

CavMan passed by classroom buildings
and walked past the Old Dorms
where students live.

A girl who lives inside waved,
"Hello CavMan!"

It was almost time for the football game.
As CavMan walked to the stadium,
he passed by some alumni.

The alumni remembered CavMan
from when they went to The University.
They said, "Hello, again, CavMan!"

Finally, CavMan arrived at Scott Stadium.

As he rode his horse, Sabre,
onto the football field, CavMan cheered,
"Let's Go 'Hoos!"

CavMan watched the game from the sidelines and cheered for the team.

The Cavaliers scored six points!
The quarterback shouted,
"Touchdown CavMan!"

At half-time the band performed
on the field.

CavMan and the crowd sang,
"The Good Old Song."

The University of Virginia Cavaliers
won the football game!

CavMan gave Coach Groh a high-five.
The coach said, "Great game CavMan!"

After the football game, CavMan
was tired. It had been a long day at
the University of Virginia.

He walked home and climbed into bed.

"Goodnight CavMan."

For Anna and Maya, Anna's friend Erica,
and all of CavMan's little fans. ~ AA

For my Mom and Dad – thank you for
supporting my dream. ~ GP

Special thanks to:

Al Groh

Steve Heon

Patricia Baughan Mickus

Jon & Courtney Szymanski

For information please contact Mascot Books,
P.O. Box 220157, Chantilly, VA 20153-0157.

ISBN: 0-9743442-3-0

Printed in the United States.

www.mascotbooks.com